QUACK, QUACK!

by Philippe Dupasquier

Ⓐ

Andersen Press
London

Copyright © 2001 by Philippe Dupasquier
The rights of Philippe Dupasquier to be identified as the author and illustrator of this work
have been asserted by him in accordance with the Copyright, Designs and Patents Act, 1988.
First published in Great Britain in 2001 by Andersen Press Ltd., 20 Vauxhall Bridge Road, London SW1V 2SA.
Published in Australia by Random House Australia Pty., 20 Alfred Street, Milsons Point, Sydney, NSW 2061.
All rights reserved. Colour separated in Switzerland by Photolitho AG, Zürich.
Printed and bound in Italy by Grafiche AZ, Verona.

10   9   8   7   6   5   4   3   2   1

British Library Cataloguing in Publication Data available.

ISBN 1 84270 015 4

This book has been printed on acid-free paper

Hello, my name is Vicki.
This is my mum and my dad
and my little brother, Ben.

We live in a lovely house on the outskirts of town.
I like playing with my little brother in our garden.

My mum loves gardening and my dad
just likes sitting in his deckchair reading
his newspaper.

The house next door used to be empty but one day
something really exciting happened . . .

A lady called Mrs Spikes moved in.
We had a new neighbour at last!

Mrs Spikes looked very nice.

She was always chatting over the hedge with Dad about the weather and giving Mum advice about gardening.

Sometimes she invited us over, me and my little brother, for a nice glass of red cordial. She said the recipe was her little secret.

One day, Mrs Spikes came back from town with a duck. It was brilliant.

She put it in the small pond she had in her garden.

"That will keep you company!" said Mum and Dad
to Mrs Spikes.
"Can my little brother and I come and feed it sometimes?"
I asked her.
It was very exciting . . .

But the next morning, we were all awakened by a strange noise. It was the quacking of Mrs Spikes' new duck.
It was very loud and it made my dad really grumpy.

The duck went on quacking all morning . . .

. . . and all afternoon.

"I expect it needs to settle down," said my mum.

But the duck did not settle down.
It went on quacking and quacking all week,
every day, and from morning to dusk.
It was dreadful!

"I can't practise my music!"
complained Ben.

"And I can't do my homework!"
I said to Mum.

In the end, Dad decided to have
a few words with Mrs Spikes
over the hedge.

"Noisy? My duck? Oh, come now, Mr Jones! It's only singing its little song. Personally, I find it very charming," she said to my dad.

But when at six o'clock on Sunday morning the duck sang "its little song" again, Dad went mad!

"This cannot go on! There must be something wrong with your duck!" he said to Mrs Spikes.

"There is nothing wrong with my duck!" she snapped back angrily. "And if you don't like it here I suggest you move somewhere else!" she added in the most horrible voice.

We couldn't believe it!

From that day on we didn't talk to her anymore.

We soon realised what kind of woman she really was.

"Did you see her driving like a maniac down our lane?" said Dad.

"And that creepy gardener she hired – always spying and laughing over the hedge," said Mum. "And the way she dresses in those dreadful old rags . . . She looks more like a witch!"

"She is a witch! We saw her through the window reading an old spell book . . ." said my little brother, ". . . and there were bats circling over that creepy tower she's got."

And what about that horrible syrup she made us drink?
"Rats' blood!" I said in a panic.
"Or squashed-up toads!" said Ben disgustingly.

"Never mind a stupid witch. I've just had an idea for a stupid duck!" said my dad one morning with a grin on his face.

QUACK
QUACK

Then he went into the garden and dug an enormous hole which he filled up with water.

After that he drove to town and came back with the biggest duck he could find which he put in the pond he'd just made.

We all thought he had gone mad!

"It's simple," he started to explain. "The noise of the two ducks is going to be unbearable and it won't be long before Mrs Spikes starts to complain . . . particularly about the duck which isn't hers!

" 'I'll get rid of my duck,' I will tell her, 'but you get rid of yours too!' "

It seemed like the perfect plan.

But the thing is that Dad's duck didn't even produce a single quack. And then to our great surprise, Mrs Spikes' duck suddenly went very quiet too! In fact both ducks kept silent all day, staring at each other through the gaps in the hedge.

"It looks as if you've found yourself a duck . . ."
said Mrs Spikes, emerging suddenly from behind the hedge
and looking almost polite.

"Yes, and it seems to like yours!" said my dad,
as politely as he could.

At last we started to enjoy the garden again, and it was great to play with our new duck.

Mrs Spikes became more chatty over the hedge and even almost nice again.

"Maybe she isn't as bad as we thought . . ." said Mum.

Of course, it was sad that the ducks were not together.

"Why don't we cut the hedge?" said my little brother.

"Yes! And make the two ponds into a big one!" I said.

Everyone thought it was a brilliant idea!

That weekend we all got together.

Mrs Spikes called on her gardener to help with the job. He turned out to be really nice and made everybody laugh with his jokes.

Mrs Spikes made sandwiches for everyone and served her secret drink. "Home-made raspberry juice," she confessed. Phew! That was a relief.

She also showed us her new bird house . . .

. . . and where she kept her
enormous stamp collection.

By the end of the day, the new pond was finished.
It was brilliant, with a large island in the middle where
the ducks happily settled down.

"Looks like the perfect ending to quite a story," said Dad
to Mrs Spikes with a smile.

But there was still one surprise to come . . .

One morning Ben and I discovered a beautiful egg, sitting right between the two ducks.

Everyone came to admire it and everyone cheered. Now this was definitely the happiest ending of all.

Or so we thought, until . . .

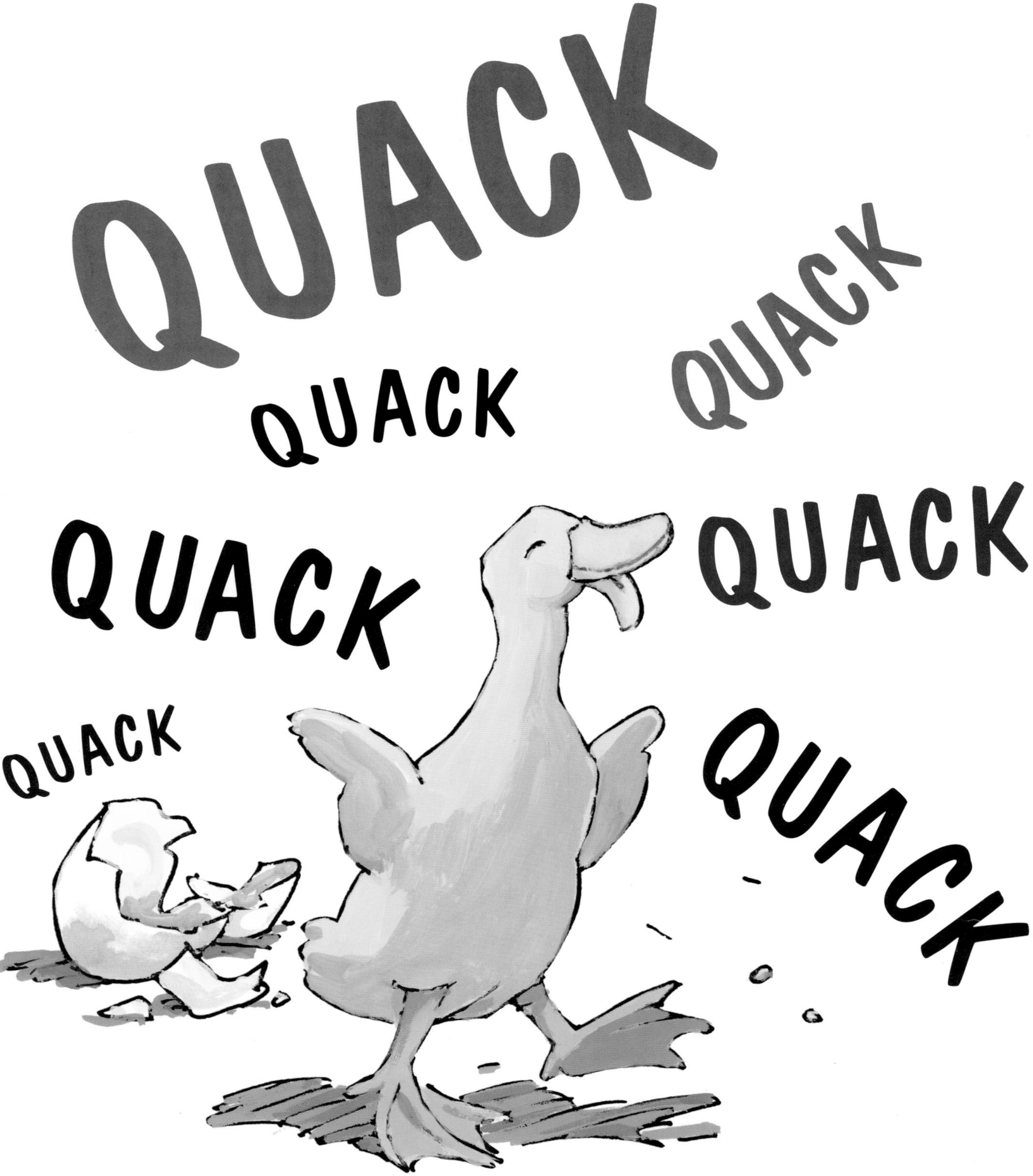
QUACK
QUACK
QUACK
QUACK
QUACK
QUACK
QUACK